GRINZA'S ORCHARD

An Enchanted Tale
by Leonard I. Eckhaus

ABOUT THE AUTHOR
LEONARD I. ECKHAUS

Leonard Eckhaus is the founder of *AFCOM*, the leading association in the world for Data Center Managers; he established and presided over *The Data Center Institute*, a think tank of leading computer industry corporate and data center visionaries; and he created, produced and published *DCM,* an award-winning magazine in the computer industry. His comments about the growth and impact of Data Centers have appeared in such major publications as *The Wall Street Journal*, *The New York Times*, the *Washington Post*, *U.S. News & World Report*, *Bloomberg News* and others.

In 2017 Leonard co-founded *LL Music,* a music production company and record label. He received two Grammy nominations in 2018 for his first album, *Rendezvous*, featuring the singer *Clint Holmes.*

His first book, *My Journey: (Lessons I've Learned Along the Way), the Memoirs of Leonard I. Eckhaus*, was published in 2018 and received several five-star reviews.

Leonard has served on the Boards of the *Nevada Ballet Theater* and the *Las Vegas Philharmonic*. He and his wife Linda are Capstone contributors at Las

Vegas' *Smith Center for the Performing Arts*. They also support the *Las Vegas Opera* and the local *Chamber Music Society*.

Leonard is married to his childhood sweetheart, Linda, for 58 years. They have two children, Lee and Jill, and three grandchildren, Stephen, Mikki and Hannah. He and his wife have been living in Las Vegas for the past twenty years.

DEDICATION

I dedicate this book to my parents, Sidney and Hortense Eckhaus, who provided me with all the advantages of a truly warm, loving family and a wonderful, magical childhood. And to all the children of the universe who, in their unique innocence add so much magic to our often-troubled adult world.

I also dedicate this work to my wife Linda, whose encouragement for me to be all I can, has never wavered and has allowed me to dream even grander dreams than I could ever imagine.

Leonard I. Eckhaus

CAST OF CHARACTERS
IN ORDER OF APPEARANCE

Cura Lovell
Danior Lovell
Grinza Lovell Roşu
Noah Hearne
Angelica Vladua
Clopin Rosu
The Guru Sylvanus
Auntie Anselina
Patrick Bogdan
Lina Bogdan
Gilli Bogdan
Natalia Rosu
Elijah Rosu
Constable Jack
Dena Petrescu
Cura Rosu
Neslson Rosu
Patin Rosu
Pali Young

GLOSSARY OF [GYPSY] TERMS

Bani	Money
Crowning	A traditional wedding ceremony where the bride and groom are 'crowned' as King and Queen of their new family unit
Cimbalom	A musical instrument, similar to a xylophone
Dadus	Father
Dai	Mother
Drabengro	Medicine Man/Woman (Healer)
Dukkering	Fortune Telling
Magick	Magic
Spirit Channelers	Those with the power to divine certain qualities upon another, such as their offspring

TABLE OF CONTENTS

INTRODUCTION

GYPSIES HAVE ALWAYS BEEN A FASCI-
NATING PEOPLE, and because they have been
responsible for the spread of so much occult knowl-
edge over so many centuries, they have often been
called *The Keepers of the Ancient Mysteries.*

By 1887 it is estimated that there were over
200,000 gypsies living in Romania. Most had been
slaves until their liberation in 1885. As a free people they wandered from town to town, trying to
find a more permanent home, but were never welcomed or treated well by the local communities.
They were viewed as outsiders and troublemak-
ers. Often, they were forced to pitch their tents on
the outskirts of the town. In many cases, the local
residents treated the gypsies so poorly that they
were forced to move away and again wander the
hills and valleys until they came upon another town
where they hoped they might be accepted.

Because they were an unwelcome people, some
created their own small villages, the largest of
which was Cojasca located in Dambovita County,
in southern Romania. And it was in this small village, nestled below Moldoveanu Peak, the highest
mountain peak in Romania, that in the year 1890
a daughter was born unto Cura and Danior Lovell.

CURA LOVELL'S
CRYSTAL BALL

CHAPTER ONE

THE LOVELLS

THE LOVELLS WERE QUITE POOR and earned their meager income as fortune tellers. One of their few possessions was a very old crystal ball that had been in Cura's family for many generations and been handed down from mother to daughter for hundreds of years.

Fortune telling, called *dukkering* was a woman's role among the gypsies. Cura had watched her mother very closely over the years as she performed the fortune telling ritual, crouched over a crystal ball in the darkened tent they called home. She remembered that her mother called herself a *clairvoyant*.

When someone wanted their fortune to be told or had a specific question about the future, they would enter the tent, cross her mother's palm with coins (in payment) and sit down in front of the rickety table on which rested the cloudy, almost eerie, ancient crystal ball.

Before the reading, her mom would have a brief conversation with the person, asking questions to get to know him or her better. As they chatted, her mother would brew a special herbal tea, allowing the aromatic vapors to flow throughout the tent. This had a very calming effect and made the reading a more spiritual experience.

When the aroma filled the tent, Cura's mother would end the conversion and crouch her head quite close to the crystal ball. Her eyes would close for a minute or so, and then she would suddenly sit up straight in her chair and begin speaking, looking straight ahead, eyes wide open, staring as if in a trance.

Typically, she would start out by saying, "I see a great change coming into your life…" and then go on using the information she had garnered in their discussion to make predictions that she knew would make the client happy.

Cura knew that someday she too would use that crystal ball to tell fortunes, so she watched her mother carefully, studying everything she did and said to her clients.

The first few times Cura herself had attempted *dukkering* she had been very nervous, but as she held more and more of these crystal ball readings, she gained confidence and became very good at it.

Cura and Danior were in their early thirties. They lived in a very old, two-room cabin. One room contained all their possessions including a bed, a small table, two chairs and an old chest of drawers that held their clothing. A small mirror hung on the wall nearest the only window in the home. The other, smaller, room was used for the fortune telling. This room's only furniture was a small table on which sat the crystal ball and two chairs, one in front of the table and the other behind it. The room was purposely kept rather dark, with only the light of a single candle illuminating the area when a reading was being done.

In the winter they burned logs in their fireplace for warmth, and in the summer, they had no relief at all from the excruciating heat. And it is on their bed, in this, their home, that their daughter, to whom they gave the name Grinza, was born on September 20th in the year 1890.

Grinza was a beautiful baby and even as a young child, Cura and Danior could see that she was very bright. This came as no surprise to them because, as *spirit channelers*, the Lovells, upon her birth, had divined upon Grinza the virtues of wisdom and beauty. And it was obvious to all that this was a very special child.

Once Grinza was born, Danior realized that their cabin was too small for the three of them. With his experience in woodworking he was able to add an additional room with its own window, to the cabin. He also built a crib, a bed and a dresser so that when Grinza was old enough to be in a separate room, they would be ready.

FOR GRINZA'S FIFTH BIRTHDAY, her parents planted a cherry tree in their front yard and gave it to her as a birthday present, telling her that if she took care of it, the tree would provide her with delicious cherries for the rest of her life.

Grinza was so excited to have her own tree! "Dadus," (as she called her father), "Dai,", (as she called her mom), "I am so happy. I love you both."

Grinza cherished that tree and was so proud, four years later, when it began to bloom and then produce fruit. Every year in late spring, the cherries would be ready and Grinza would pick them. There were so many cherries that Grinza would bring some to each of her friends and relatives. And she enjoyed how happy everyone was when they tasted their sweetness.

BY THE TIME GRINZA WAS FOURTEEN her cherry tree had fully matured and was producing the biggest, juiciest cherries in the whole village. She spent some time every day picking the ripest cherries and cleaning up the ground under the tree where a small number of leaves and cherries had fallen.

She was already aware of boys and found herself attracted to several in her village. In fact, one young man, Noah Hearne, told her he liked her, but she turned him down when he wanted to walk her home. There was something about him that just didn't sit right with Grinza. Most of her friends were married by the time they were fifteen - marriages that had been arranged by their parents. She knew that her parents would soon pick a suitor for her, and she worried about whom that might be. She sure wouldn't be happy if it was Noah.

Every day Grinza spent a minute looking at her reflection in the mirror by the window. "If only I was beautiful," she thought, "maybe a more handsome man would want me."

ALTHOUGH HER PARENTS OFTEN TOLD HER that she was beautiful, she didn't really believe it. For one thing, Grinza had freckles and she was convinced that her freckles made her ugly. So, she would look in the mirror and wonder if it were possible to get rid of them.

Grinza had confided her concerns about her freckles to her best friend, Angelica Vladua. Angelica was a year older than Grinza and at fifteen years old, was nervous and excited about whom her parents might find as a suiter for her. She had heard them talking about it one night when they thought she was already asleep.

Angelica and Grinza often sat under Grinza's cherry tree and whispered about whom they might marry. One thing for sure – they both wanted strong, handsome husbands.

There was one young man named Clopin who had smiled at Grinza several times as they passed each other in the village and seemed like he wanted to approach her, but he was simply too shy. "Just as well." thought Grinza, He would be handsome though, she thought, if he too, didn't have so many freckles.

Grinza had heard that high up on the nearest mountain, their clan's spiritual leader, the Guru Sylvanus, lived in isolation, only interacting with the clan when serious problems necessitated his involvement. It was said that his power was so great that he could do anything, grant any wish. It was also said that he observed everything going on in the village, even from a distance, and knew what lurked in each of the villager's hearts. He knew who lived peaceful and meaningful lives and who could not be trusted.

Grinza thought that she might go to the Guru and ask for his help in getting rid of her freckles, but no one was allowed to visit him without an invitation. She hated her freckles, but just didn't know what to do.

AUNTIE ANSELINA

CHAPTER TWO

AUNTIE ANSELINA

ONE DAY, Angelica told Grinza that she had heard that in their village, there lived a wise old witch, a *Drabengro* – a woman named Auntie Anselina, who had conjured many spells to heal and help the local villagers. In fact, Angelica told her that it was rumored that this Auntie Anselina was very close with the Guru Sylvanus.

That afternoon, as she and Angelica sat beneath the cherry tree, Grinza told her that she had decided to visit Auntie Anselina and ask for her help. When she got up and began to walk home, Noah Hearne approached her. "I overheard you telling Angelica that you are going to visit Auntie Anselina," he said. "I've heard that she can be very mean and can put a spell on you that will haunt you for the rest of your life."

And with that, Noah's eyes narrowed and, with a sneer on his face, he hissed, "I'm warning you – you'd better be careful!" "I'm not afraid," she told him. "You're just trying to scare me." And, the very next day Grinza gathered up all her courage and went to visit her.

AUNTIE ANSELINA LIVED IN A CRUDE TENT, with only a flap for a door. When Grinza arrived at the tent she hesitated, her heart pounding so loudly she thought it would burst. But she had come all this way, so, with much trepidation, she called into the tent, "Auntie Anselina, it is I, Grinza Lovell. May I come in? I have a very important question for you."

At first, Grinza heard no reply, but after a moment's silence, a voice, almost a whisper, from within the tent answered, "Come in, my dear, and don't be afraid."

Grinza pulled back the flap and glanced inside the tent. It was a small space, with a cot, a small table and four chairs. To the left of the table, in a rocking chair, sat an old woman with gray hair pulled into a bun. She had wrinkles, more like cracks, etched into her face, but she was smiling and that made Grinza a bit more comfortable. The only jewelry she had on was a gold ring with a very deep green stone.

"COME IN SO I CAN SEE YOU, DEAR GRINZA, and sit down so we can talk." offered Auntie Anselina, motioning Grinza to a chair by the table. "What is it you have come to ask me?"

As she worked up the courage to ask about getting rid of her freckles, Grinza held out a bowl filled with her bright red cherries. "I… I brought these for you." she stammered. Then she noticed the beautiful ring on Auntie Anselina's finger and told her how lovely it was. "Thank you," she said, "it is an emerald and it was given to me by the Guru Sylvanus, for helping him end the drought of 1887 when there was not even enough water to drink. We prayed together for rain, and soon it came – great gushing rains that saved the whole clan."

Grinza was really impressed. If Anselina had prayed together with the Guru and helped save the village, she must also have great powers.

"Auntie Anselina," Grinza began, "I am fourteen years old and soon my parents will be finding a suitor for me." Embarrassed, she looked down at the floor and continued, "Perhaps if I could somehow be made beautiful, a more handsome man might want me."

Grinza lifted her head and gazed at Auntie Anselina. Touching the freckles on her face, she added, "If only you could help me get rid of these freckles. Is that possible?"

And Auntie Anselina replied, "I am an old woman and have conjured spells and other elements to help neighbors many times over the years. But there is no spell I can conjure to do what you ask."

Tears ran down Grinza's face as she whispered, "Does that mean there is no hope for me?"

"Well," the old woman replied, "there is one thing you can try. It has worked for some."

"Please, please tell me," Grinza begged. "I will do anything."

Then the old gypsy told her that if she would gather the youngest leaves from an elm tree right after it rained, or when the morning dew was still on them, and draw the wet leaves gently over her face leaving the liquid to dry on its own, the freckles might disappear.

Grinza couldn't wait to tell Angelica. She hugged the old woman and left for home, arriving after dark, and when asked, lying to Cura about where she'd been.

THE VERY NEXT MORNING GRINZA WOKE UP EARLY. She was excited. She threw her clothes on and ran outside. She knew that there was a stately elm tree just down the street and she raced right to it. As she approached the tree she stopped and looked up. There were no branches low enough for her to reach. She had forgotten about that.

Grinza examined the wide, almost smooth trunk and realized she wouldn't be able to climb it. There was nowhere to get a foothold and the lowest branch was at least ten feet above the ground.

Finally, she had an idea. She ran home, found a long piece of rope and brought it back to the tree. She tried several times to swing the rope over the lowest branch so she could pull it down and pick off some leaves, and by her third try, she was finally able to do it. Pulling hard on the rope, she lowered the branch down to a level she could reach and get some leaves. Then Grinza slowly loosened the rope until the branch rose back to its normal height.

Just as she was about to go, with the still damp-ened leaves in her hand, she saw that young man, Clopin, walking down the path that ran beside the trees. "Not now," she thought, "don't try speaking to me right now." And, luckily, he didn't. He just smiled at her as always and walked on by.

She quickly carried the rope and the damp leaves to a small clearing about thirty feet behind the road where no one would be able to see her. After looking around to be sure no one else was in sight, Grinza sat down and very carefully drew the leaves over her face, covering all her freckles with the moisture. Then she sat there until her face completely dried. She was very excited to go home and look at her new face in the mirror but forced herself to wait until her parents had gone for the day, so she could be alone in the house.

When she was comfortable that her parents would be gone, Grinza went back to her house, entered, and stood before the mirror with her eyes closed. She whispered a short prayer out loud, then holding her breath, she slowly opened her eyes. At first, she thought the freckles were gone, but that was just her mind playing tricks. As her eyes began to focus, she could see that nothing on her face had changed. She still had all her freckles. Grinza just stood there, looking at the image of her face in the mirror, and cried.

GRINZA DIDN'T HAVE MANY PERSONAL POSSESSIONS. She had a nice hand-carved wooden hairbrush, a few pretty articles of clothing that she wore on special occasions, and her cherry tree. And it was the cherry tree that she loved the most - this tree that she had nurtured from as far back in her life as she could remember — the tree to which she had whispered so many of her hopes and dreams, the tree that brought her delicious, sweet cherries each season. It was her pride and joy. She even managed to keep some of the cherries through the winter by making a few jars of cherry marmalade.

TWO YEARS WENT BY and Grinza's parents never brought up the idea of an arranged marriage, even though that was still the tradition that most of the Gypsies followed. And, at sixteen years old, by which time most of her friends were already married, Cura and Danior still hadn't put any pressure on her about it.

Grinza's best friend, Angelica was already married to a young man who was the only shoemaker in the village. Although this marriage had been brokered by her parents, Angelica seemed very happy.

Grinza wondered why her own parents hadn't tried to arrange a marriage for her, but she was afraid to broach the subject for fear it would lead to them doing just that. Until one evening when Cura and Danior sat her down for a serious discussion about her future.

Grinza looked at her parents and could sense that what they were about to say would be very important. The look on Danior's face told her that they had made an important decision – an important decision about her! His face was stoic, very serious; however, she could also see a slight smile forming on her mother's mouth, relieving some of Grinza's tension.

Cura began. "Grinza," she said, "as you know, our gypsy tradition is for us, your parents, to arrange a marriage for you. It has been this way for a thousand years. And you may have wondered why, by your age, we have not yet arranged for such a union."

She went on, "Your father and I have thought long and hard about this, the most important event that will happen in your life. We love you so much and want you to be happy, and therefore we are willing to forgo an arranged marriage for you – but only for one more year. If you find someone and fall in love with him during that time, we will be so happy for you."

"But," "added Danior, "If you are not engaged or married one year from now, we will have to obey the traditions that all our ancestors have held to over the years and arrange a marriage for you."

Giving her this opportunity was unheard of among the gypsies in their village and Grinza couldn't contain the joy she felt at that moment. "*Dai, Dadus*, I love you so much, and I am so grateful for this opportunity. Thank you, thank you." And with that she rushed into their outstretched arms and all three held each other around and hugged.

As summer stretched into fall that year, Noah Hearne often approached Grinza, asking to walk her somewhere or just talk to her, but Grinza had already heard rumors about his bullying other boys and getting into fights with them, and she didn't want to have him around. Finally, she just said, "Noah Hearne, I know all about you. Just stay away from me!" And, when she told him that, his anger exploded and he lifted his fists as if to strike her but stopped just short of that and turning around, shouted "You'll be sorry!' as he ran away.

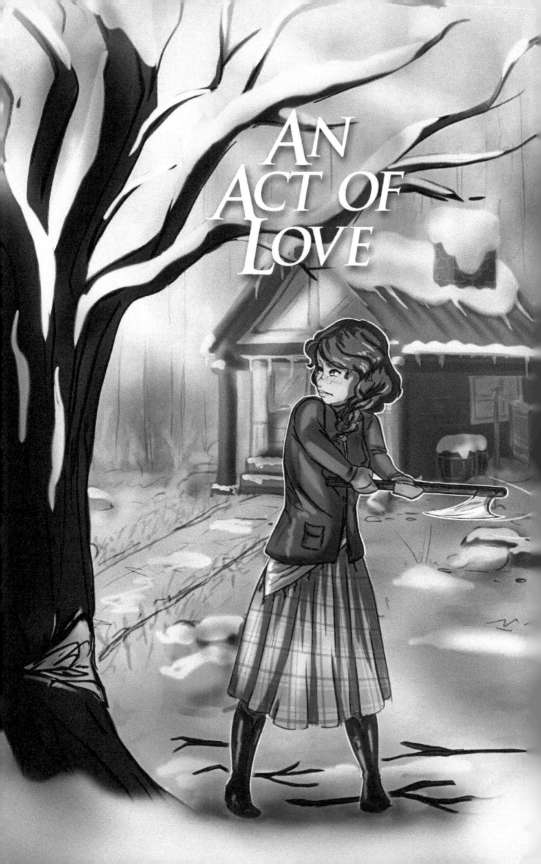

CHAPTER THREE

GRINZA'S SACRIFICE

THAT WINTER, THE WINTER OF 1906 was the coldest ever experienced in Romania. There was little food because everything was frozen, and not much wood for the fireplace because everyone was using so much of it. The poor people living in Cojasca had cut down most of the trees in the neighborhood, just to have firewood. Because of the constant cold, many were getting sick, some dying.

Grinza became really frightened when both of her parents came down with the same illness that had left so many other people in their village bed-ridden, and even worse. They both coughed and had constant chills. They didn't have a lot of food, and when they did try to eat, they would have stomach cramps and throw up. One evening Grinza went to add a log to the fireplace and found they had just one left.

Unless she could find a way to keep them warm and nurse them back to health, Grinza knew her parents wouldn't survive. She was desperate but couldn't think of any way to help them… until finally she realized what she had to do and the sacrifice she had to make.

SHE HAD TO SAVE HER PARENTS, and the only way to do that was to give up her single greatest possession – her cherry tree, whose trunk and branches had grown greatly over the years and could be used as the firewood she so desperately needed. Using her prized cherry tree as firewood was the only way to keep the cabin warm.

Grinza went to a nearby shed where her father kept the few tools he had and picked up an axe. In a daze, a sort of trance, she carried it to the cherry tree, gazed up at its branches and began to cry. "I do love you," she said to the tree. "But I have to do this." And, with tears streaming down her cheeks, Grinza began to chop.

With each swing of the axe, Grinza cried harder and harder, to the point where she had to stop and wipe her eyes so she could see well enough to continue. She remembered all the wonderful moments she had spent with the tree, grooming it, picking the cherries, raking the leaves. She remembered how every day she would wake up with a smile, ready to run out and visit her tree and, silly as it sounded, say "Good morning, tree. It's another glorious day." She had to save her parents and to do that she had to give up her most precious possession. Life wasn't fair. But she continued chopping.

As she chopped, she could feel the wind blowing and the flakes of the winter's first snow wetting her face. Her tears were beginning to freeze on her cheeks. A chill went through her and she shivered. With each stroke of the axe she got more and more tired, her muscles begging her to stop. The love and tender care she had given her tree for all these years had allowed it to grow a wide and strong trunk.

ALMOST TWO WEEKS WENT BY and Grinza had been able to keep the cabin warm enough for her parents to begin to recover. They could now hold down the little food Grinza had been able to get, by trading some of her wood for food. The cherry tree that she so loved, that had given sweet fruit to her for so many years, had now given new life and sustenance to her family.

As Cura and Danior regained some of their strength and energy, Grinza was able to get more rest. She still did all the cleaning, but they could eat and wash themselves and Cura again began to do some of the cooking.

Winter came and went, and the warmth of spring entered the village. Flowers began to bloom, the birds and other animals were once again seen on the roads and fields, and life returned to normal.

Grinza didn't know it, but word of her act of sacrificing her most prized possession in order to save her parents that winter, had spread throughout the village and beyond.

ONE DAY, WHILE SHE WAS WASHING THE BREAKFAST DISHES, Grinza received a summons from Auntie Anselina. She was asked to come to her tent and bring clothing for several days. Together they were to travel to Moldoveanu Peak, where they would meet with Silvanus, the Guru.

When she told her parents, they were both excited. In their village, an invitation from Silvanus was the highest honor one could receive. They couldn't wait to let their friends and neighbors know. Their daughter, Grinza, upon whom they had divined the channels of wisdom and beauty, was, even at this early age, being recognized as someone very special in their community.

Early the next morning, Grinza kissed her parents goodbye, and left to meet Auntie Anselina at her tent. It was a cool morning on a beautiful spring day. The air was crisp and invigorating to Grinza as she walked along the way, wondering why she had been so chosen. And as she walked, she again passed that boy Clopin who, as always, smiled at her but didn't stop to talk.

WHEN SHE ARRIVED AT THE TENT, she found Auntie Anselina standing outside, ready to leave, her overnight bundle on the ground beside her. They hugged and started walking together toward whatever adventure lay before them.

As they walked along, Grinza asked, "Do you know why I have been summoned by Silvanus? I wanted to bring him a special gift, but I have no gold or jewelry. I did bring the only thing I have, which is a single jar of cherry marmalade I had been saving. Now I wonder if I should have even brought it – it is such a meager offering."

To which Anselina answered, "It is customary to bring a gift, and its value is not measured in *bani* (money). It is the thought itself that is important.

A while later, Auntie Anselina told Grinza that she needed to stop for a rest. They found a nice area of grass about twenty feet off the road and sat down under a shady tree. They started to talk, but Auntie Anselina soon stretched out and fell asleep.

GRINZA DECIDED TO TAKE A LITTLE WALK while Auntie Anselina slept. She started to follow a narrow path that led straight into the woods and soon found herself at a fork and had to decide which way to go. As she was about to take the path to the right, she thought she heard a noise coming from somewhere up ahead along the path to the left. Curious, she walked towards the noise which she began to recognize as the sound of someone crying.

In a few more minutes the path led Grinza to a clearing where she saw a small boy about ten years old, lying on the ground with a large shard of glass embedded in his thigh. "Hello," she said, "my name is Grinza and I'm going to try and help you. Don't be afraid."

She approached the boy and could see that he was bleeding pretty badly, and in a lot of pain. She bent down and carefully grasped the piece of glass between her thumb and forefinger. "This might hurt, but I have to do it." she told the boy, and pulled it out; unfortunately, with the glass removed, the bleeding got even worse. Grinza took off the scarf she was wearing and tied it tightly around the boy's thigh above the incision. This stopped the bleeding and the boy, still sobbing thanked her.

"How did this happen?" she asked.

"I was out for the same walk that I take every day and was carrying a bottle of water to drink, when I tripped on a rock and fell. The bottle somehow broke and the piece of glass went into my leg."

"What's your name?" Grinza asked, "And do you live around here?"

"Patrick," the boy answered, "and, yes I live over that hill behind you."

Grinza helped him get up, first to his knees, then up on both legs. And with her arm wrapped around him for support, they slowly began walking up the hill.

AUNTIE ANSELINA AWOKE TO THE SOUND OF A HORSE'S HOOVES clip-clopping on the dirt roadway. She opened her eyes and half-awake, saw the man on the horse bring the animal to a halt about ten feet from where she lay.

He had a full beard and long unruly hair. He was sweating and looked dirty, in need of a bath. When he got close enough, she could smell both the horse and the man.

Auntie Anselina was frightened but didn't want the man to know that.

He was dressed in a green shirt covered by a brown vest with one green ribbon pulled around his waist, and a bandanna tied around his head. All his clothing was stained with sweat and what looked like wine.

"What are you doing out here all alone?" the man asked. "There are bad people in this area. You are lucky that it is I who found you and not someone else who might want to harm you."

Auntie Anselina pulled her overnight bag and Grinza's case closer to her. "What do you want?" she asked.

BY NOW, GRINZA AND PATRICK had reached the crest of the hill and were beginning to descend, walking slowly towards a small log cabin about halfway down the path.

It was getting chilly and Grinza wished she still had on her scarf but was happy she had been able to use it to stop the boy's bleeding. She could see smoke coming up from the cabin's chimney and was glad they were almost there.

A few minutes later they were in front of the cabin and Patrick called out to his mother inside. "I'm back," he yelled from outside the front door, "and I had an accident."

In a moment, Patrick's mom threw open the front door and came running out. She stopped short when she saw Grinza, but asked Patrick if he was okay before addressing the stranger. "I'm okay." answered Patrick. "I tripped and my water bottle broke and cut my leg. This is Grinza and she helped stop the bleeding and half carried me home."

"Thank you for helping him," offered Patrick's mom. "I'm Lina Bogdan and my husband Gilli is in the house. Please come in."

THE MAN TOLD AUNTIE ANSELINA THAT HE WASN'T GOING TO HURT HER... if she did what he asked. Then he asked her what she had in the two bundles beside her. "Just clothes and a little food." she answered, angry at the impertinence of this man.

The man reached over and picked up one of the bags. Opening it, he saw that all it contained was some clothing, a loaf of bread for her to eat along the way, and some fruit. He then grabbed the second bag and found that it also contained nothing of value. He looked at Auntie Anselina and snorted. "Do you have any money?" to which an indignant Auntie Anselina replied, "No, I do not. But I do have many friends who would come looking for you if you dared to rob me."

The man turned around and threw the bag he was holding, onto the ground. It was at this moment, while his back was turned that Auntie Anselina struggled to her feet, pushed him down and began to run away from him.

PATRICK'S PARENTS, LINA AND GILLI offered Grinza some water, which she gratefully accepted. "What are you doing out here all by yourself?" asked Gilli. "This is not a good area in which to be out alone. There are thieves roaming these hills. Thieves who would rob you and do you harm."

Then Grinza told them where she was going and that she was not alone. "In fact," she said, "I should be getting back to Auntie Anselina right away. If she wakes up and doesn't see me, she'll be worried."

"Then you should go, but I can't let you go alone." said Gilli. "I'm going with you to be sure you are okay." And a few minutes later Grinza and Gilli began their trek back to find Auntie Anselina.

THE MAN QUICKLY GOT UP. He turned toward Auntie Anselina and saw that she had begun running away. Infuriated, he started to chase after her. At her age, Auntie Anselina couldn't run very fast and the man quickly caught up with her. As soon as he grabbed her, he pulled a length of rope from his pocket and tied her hands together behind her. Then he walked her back to the clearing, sat her down alongside the two bags she had left behind and tied her legs together so she couldn't run away again. "If you try anything like that again, I'll hurt you." He snarled.

When the man had been tying her hands, he noticed the beautiful and obviously valuable ring she was wearing. Now that she was tied up and laying on the grass, the man told her to roll over on her stomach, so he could get at the ring.

GRINZA AND GILLI GOT TO WHERE THE FORK IN THE ROAD began and heard a man's voice coming from the clearing where she had left Auntie Anselina. They both started running and in about a minute they could see the man up ahead, and Auntie Anselina tied up, and laying on her stomach. Gilli motioned to Grinza for her to stop where she was and to be quiet.

Slowly and stealthily Gilli walked to the edge of the clearing, stopping only about ten feet away from the man whose back was towards him. As the man took the ring off Auntie Anselina's finger, he heard him saying, "What a beautiful ring. I'll bet I can get a lot of money for it."

Gilli knew that with the man's back to him, he had to strike now. From his front pocket he pulled out the hunk of wood that he always carried with him for protection and ran to the man, who heard him and started to turn around.

Gilli closed in on the man so fast that he had no time to react. He hit him in the head and the man fell down. He was knocked out and Gilli stood over him, making sure he wouldn't be getting up right away. Then he turned to Auntie Anselina. "Are you alright?" he asked her, as he bent down to untie first her legs and then her hands. "I'm fine," she answered. "He was trying to steal my ring. I'm so glad you got here just in time."

Grinza, hearing this, ran to them, hugging Auntie Anselina. I'm so glad you're okay," she said, and then, in a rush of words, told her what had happened on her walk and how she had met Patrick, Lina and Gilli. Gilli now offered to walk with them to the foot of the mountain, and they left immediately, Grinza and Auntie Anselina eager to get to Sylvanus.

THE GURU SYLVANUS

CHAPTER FOUR

THE GURU SYLVANUS

ONCE THEY REACHED THE FOOT OF THE MOUNTAIN, Gilli hugged them goodbye and started back home.

It was a three-hour climb to the cave in which the Guru Sylvanus lived. And when they arrived, they stopped at the entrance and peeked inside.

The cave was sparsely furnished. Sitting on a large pillow near the firepit, the Guru Sylvanus welcomed them. "Please, please come in," he said. "I have been expecting you both."

APPROACHING HIM AND NOT KNOWING WHAT ELSE TO DO, Grinza held out her jar of cherry marmalade and offered it to Sylvanus, who took it with both hands and held it before his face. As the women watched, tears streamed down Sylvanus's cheeks.

He stared at the jar for another moment, then lifted his eyes to Grinza and said, "This is a very special gift. I know what your cherry tree meant to you and the sacrifice you made. That is why I have sent for you. I am an old man now but have been given a gift from the ancients. It is the gift of *magick.* And because of what you have given of yourself, because of the beauty you carry within you, I wish to grant you one wish. You must choose it tonight after we have eaten dinner. And you must choose it wisely and not waste it."

A little later, when Sylvanus went for his afternoon walk, Grinza said to Auntie Anselina, "I am not so young now as I was when I first came to see you. I no longer care so much about my freckles – they are part of who I am. My wish today is for my parents to have many more happy, healthy years ahead, and for me to find the right husband and have a family of my own. I have no desire for great wealth. I really don't know what I might ask for."

GRINZA DIDN'T KNOW WHAT TO DO. That evening, a lavish meal was set before them, but she was so nervous that she had trouble even holding her fork steady. Her hand shook as she took a drink from her glass of water and she quickly put it back on the table. She hoped no one saw her trembling.

She knew that Sylvanus could grant any wish she might ask for, but there was really nothing important she was missing in her life.

AFTER THEY HAD EATEN, Sylvanus asked Grinza what wish he might grant her. Grinza looked at him, then looked at Auntie Anselina. Both were gazing directly at her, waiting to hear what she would say.

After a moment's silence, during which Grinza gathered up her courage, she responded thoughtfully. "I know I have to choose, but I have very mixed emotions." She went on to explain that she wasn't interested in riches or jewelry – that to be happy she just wanted a man she loved and to have a family of her own. "At this point in my life," she said, "I realize the importance of my friends and family. They are what truly make me happy." She also told him of her one-time desire to be rid of her freckles and how silly that seemed to her now. "I think," she said, "that everything I need to make me happy, is already within myself. I can and will make that happen." "So," she ended, "I already have everything I really want, and I have no need to ask for anything else."

"Perhaps," offered Sylvanus, "perhaps I can still do something for you." And, with that cryptic remark, they all settled down to a good night's sleep. The next morning, Grinza and Auntie Anselina hugged the Guru Sylvanus goodbye and began their trek home.

AFTER LEAVING ANSELINA AT HER TENT, Grinza walked to her house. She was somehow already feeling good about her encounter with Sylvanus, when she approached her house and stopped short. She was stunned by what was going on in her front yard!

There, in the exact spot that her cherry tree had once stood, was another, fully mature, cherry tree. And below it both of her parents, along with another young man, were picking cherries off the tree and putting them in baskets.

When her mom looked up and saw her, she exclaimed, "Grinza, it is a miracle. It is a new cherry tree where yesterday there was nothing but grass and dirt. Somehow, Grinza, your cherry tree is back!"

"Come here, come here," shouted her father, "I want to introduce you to Clopin Rosu. He lives with his parents, just down the street, and he has offered to help harvest the cherries."

WITH THAT, GRINZA CAME FORWARD and smiled as she shook hands with Clopin and looked closely at his face. He, the very same young man who always smiled at her when their paths crossed, like Grinza, also had a face full of freckles. And, yes, he was so handsome.

… And Grinza knew what the Guru Sylvanus had done, and she was happy. Oh, so happy.

CHAPTER FIVE

CLOPIN ASKS FOR GRINZA'S HAND

THREE MONTHS HAD GONE BY since the miraculous discovery of the new cherry tree in the exact same spot that the tree Grinza had chopped down to save her parents, had once stood. The excitement this miracle tree had generated throughout the village spread near and far, and people spoke of Grinza in hushed tones, as a special, chosen person having been honored by none other than the Guru Sylvanus.

During these three months, Clopin had gathered enough courage to begin speaking to Grinza whenever they passed each other in the village, but he was very, very shy and approaching the young lady he was falling in love with from afar, wasn't easy for him.

He started by simply saying hello when they passed each other until one day he said his usual hello and then added, "Isn't it a beautiful day?" He not only surprised Grinza when he said that, but he even surprised himself.

Grinza had gotten used to Clopin smiling at her and saying hello each time they passed one another, and she was beginning to look forward to seeing him, so when he added, "Isn't it a beautiful day?" she found herself walking up to him and answering, "Yes it is. Are you going somewhere or are you just out for a walk?" And that was the start of a wonderful relationship.

CLOPIN TOLD HIS PARENTS, NATALIA AND ELIJAH ROSU, about Grinza and they were pleased for him. They knew of Grinza because everyone in the village knew of the magical cherry tree and how Grinza had been favored by the Guru Sylvanus. They also knew how shy Clopin was and secretly hoped his feelings for Grinza would overcome that, and they encouraged him to pursue the relationship if that's what he wanted.

GRINZA'S MOM, CURA, AND HER DAD, DANIOR, were very pleased that she had found someone she really liked. Clopin worked in the village as a handyman fixing broken tools, helping build cabins and whatever else needed doing. He was a very good carpenter and was offered more jobs building furniture than he could handle. He was also saving money so he could ask Grinza to be his wife. Even at this early age, Clopin dreamed of one day owning his own furniture business.

Grinza was also working – as a tutor, helping village children learn to read and write. She loved this work and she loved the children, already dreaming about someday having her own.

For the next year, Clopin and Grinza saw each other almost every day. Often, he would bring her flowers or candy, and they delighted in taking long, slow walks in the nearby wooded area, following paths that led them to springs and waterfalls where they would sit on the grass, hold hands and talk about their dreams and hopes for the future.

By this time, they both realized that they were deeply in love with one another and wanted to get engaged. One Saturday morning, Clopin approached Danior alone in his cabin, and asked him for his daughter's hand in marriage. He told him how much in love with Grinza he was and that he had been saving money for them to build their own cabin. He promised to always take care of Grinza and that he hoped together, he and Grinza would bring many grandchildren to Cura and Danior.

Danior called Cura and Grinza to join them in the cabin. He told them what Clopin had said, and asked, first, if Cura was in favor of this union.

Cura was. She had secretly hoped for this ever since the day Clopin had first offered to help harvest the cherries from the new tree. She knew him to be a good man and a hard worker, and she would be thrilled to welcome him into their family.

She looked directly at Clopin and spoke. "I have come to know and respect you over this past year, and if this is what you and Grinza want, I will be pleased."

The only one they hadn't heard from yet was Grinza, and Danior turned to her and asked if this was what she wanted, and if she loved Clopin, to which she replied, "I love Clopin with all my heart and, yes, I want to be his wife." Then Danior gave give Grinza and Clopin his official blessing and their future was sealed, except for the traditional approval of the union by the villagers. And Danior, Cura and Grinza were all so happy that they had decided to allow Grinza the opportunity to fall in love on her own and eschew the arranged marriages to which most of the village youth were subjected.

The next morning, as she so often did, Ginza found herself sitting in the shade under her cherry tree. And as was her wont, she began speaking to it. "I'm going to get married!" she yelled to her tree. And, in this way, the tree shared in this special joy.

THERE WAS SO MUCH PLANNING TO DO before the wedding, but before they could do anything else, by tradition, they had to get the approval for this marriage from the villagers.

To do this, Grinza's parents sent the following open invitation to the entire village:

*"Cura and Danior Lovell, together with
Natalia and Elijah Rosu,*

*seek approval for their children, Grinza and
Clopin, to become engaged. You are invited
to join us in the village square this Saturday
evening at 6:00 pm for food and drink. As
always, all who are in favor of this union are
asked to wear a red scarf. Those opposed
should wear a black."*

THE WHOLE VILLAGE WAS EXCITED. It wasn't every day that there was a new engagement to celebrate. Everyone got out their best clothes and made sure that their red scarves were clean. If the villagers approved, as all expected they would, the engagement would become official that evening.

Saturday was almost upon them and the Lovells and the Rosus had a lot to do. Cura and Natalie cooked cakes and pies. They gathered vegetables from their gardens to make several different salads. And the men went to hunt the pheasants that they would prepare over an open flamed pit they dug in the ground. Wine and Russian vodka would be brought by each of the villagers who attended, and the music provided by two friends of the family, one playing the violin and the other on the *cimbalom* (very similar to a xylophone).

IN ONE HOME, HOWEVER, not everyone was happy or looking forward to the party. Not everyone was happy that Grinza was getting engaged to Clopin. Noah Hearne, who had been turned down by Grinza a few years ago, when he told her he liked her, was very unhappy. When he and his parents got dressed for the party, he found a black scarf and put it in his pocket so his parents wouldn't see it. Only adults could vote on the engagement. Children were not expected to wear a scarf at all.

The villagers began arriving a few minutes before 6:00 pm. By 6:30 almost the entire village was gathered in the square to celebrate the coming engagement. Everyone seemed to be wearing red scarves, in favor of the couple going forward with their engagement and future marriage. Once everyone had finished eating, the dancing began. Grinza's parents, along with Clopin's, were the first to get out on the dance floor, and soon many of the villagers joined them. Many sang along with the music. Everyone seemed really happy, and ready to celebrate.

After the dancing had been going on for about thirty minutes, Grinza's dad called for everyone to quiet down so he could speak. Standing alongside his wife, and with Clopin's parents and with Grinza and Clopin beside them, he began.

"Thank you all for coming tonight to endorse and welcome the engagement of our daughter

Grinza and future son-in-law, Clopin Rosu." He was about to say how pleased they were that everyone had chosen to wear a red scarf in approval of this union, when out of the corner of his eye he noticed one black scarf. Noah Hearne, whose parents he had known for years, stood to the side of the villagers and wore the black scarf. He had an angry scowl on his face and when Danior's eyes met his, the young man turned on his heels and ran away from the square where they were all gathered. It looked like he was headed towards the nearby woods.

Danior motioned for the music to start again and turned to Grinza to find out if she knew why Noah might have done that.

"Grinza," he asked, "Is there any reason that Noah would be angry that you are getting engaged to Clopin?" Grinza told her father that she had no idea. In fact, she said that they hadn't even spoken since the time she told him she wasn't interested in him as a boyfriend.

When the evening ended, Clopin and Grinza were officially engaged and could now begin making all the plans for their wedding. They were so excited as they walked home, hand in hand and said goodnight. Two young lovers dreaming of the exciting future that lay before them.

THE FIRST THING THEY HAD TO DO was select the date of the wedding. Because the traditional wedding festivities went on for three days, they needed it to be held in the summer when the temperature would be comfortable and the grass warm enough for guests to lay on blankets so they could sit down and eat or even take a nap.

They selected the weekend of August 14th, 15th and 16th when the harvesting would be completed, and when everyone had the time to just relax and enjoy themselves.

NOAH HEARNE ONCE AGAIN BECAME ANGRY when his parents received the invitation to Grinza's wedding. Why had she turned him down for Clopin? He had been nice to her, He told her he liked her. And she had the nerve to turn him away. She would be sorry. He would make sure of that.

Noah had been in and out of trouble since his early teen years. He had always been a bully and most of the boys and girls his age didn't like him. He had been caught taking money from the church's poor box and been arrested when he set fire to a friend's mailbox after they had an argument. His parents didn't know how to handle him, and they were very worried about the kind of man he would grow up to be.

AS THE WEEKS WENT BY LEADING INTO AUGUST, Grinza kept herself busy tending to her cherry tree, helping keep the house clean and spending time with Clopin. They met every day now, by her tree, and went for a long walk. They discussed their wedding plans and what it would be like for them living on their own. Most gypsy children moved in with the groom's parents when they got married, but Clopin had been saving his money and they were going to buy a cabin for themselves.

In the heat of the afternoon sun, Grinza often sat in the shade of her cherry tree and read a book. It wasn't unusual for her to spend much of the afternoon there, often accompanied by Angelica, whom she had asked to be her Matron of Honor. The two had been friends for so long, it was as if they were sisters.

The gentle breezes that swept through the cherry blossoms were a pleasant relief from the heat, and Grinza felt completely at rest and comfortable sitting there under the tree that she loved so much.

GRINZA THOUGHT ABOUT MOVING OUT FROM HER PARENT'S HOUSE, the only home she had ever known. Yes, she would still be in the village and would be able to visit as often as she liked, but it wouldn't be the same. No longer would she hear her mother singing as she brushed her hair each morning. No longer would her father kiss her on the cheek and say good morning when she came into the kitchen for breakfast. She loved them both so much and even though she would not be far, she would dearly miss the little everyday moments she spent with them. Thinking of this brought tears to her eyes, but they were tears of love and happiness as much as tears of sadness.

THE NIGHT BEFORE THE WEDDING Clopin's parents visited Cura and Danior at their cabin. With them they brought the traditional bottle of wine decorated with coins strung around it, and a wedding cake covered with a handkerchief. This food and wine, along with a small amount of money was the customary "payment" to the bride's parents for taking their daughter away. Cura and Danior opened the bottle of wine and together the parents of the engaged couple drank a toast to a lasting marriage and welcomed each other into their now expanded families. With tears of joy and happiness, they hugged each other and wished each other a good night's sleep before the festivities began the next day.

Grinza kissed her parents' good night and went to sleep realizing it would be the last night she spent in the bed she had slept in every night of her life. It was the end of an era for her, but also the beginning of a new life. She was excited and a bit frightened at the same time.

A little after midnight Grinza was awoken by a scratching sound at her window. She arose from her bed and went to the window to investigate. At the window she could see Noah Hearne outside. She opened the window and asked him what he was doing there. "Grinza," he told her, "If you marry Clopin it will be the biggest mistake you ever made. You turned me down and I'll never forgive you for that. I'll make sure you and Clopin are never happy." Grinza shut the window and returned to bed, but she couldn't get Noah out of her mind and wasn't able to fall back to sleep for a long time.

CHAPTER SIX

THE WEDDING

ON FRIDAY, AUGUST 14, 1908 THE VILLAGE WOKE UP to a bright, sunny morning, promising great weather for the wedding that had taken over everyone's excitement for the last few days. Best clothes were ironed. Money was set aside for the wedding gifts they would give to the bride and groom to help them start off their new life together. The women were getting their hair done. The men tried to rest in anticipation of a long, active weekend of drinking and dancing and celebrating. Those with small children arranged for babysitters. The mood throughout the day was jubilant.

CLOPIN AWOKE EARLY, FULL OF EXCITEMENT AND ANTICIPATION. This was it – the day he had been dreaming of, for such a long time. He wished he could go see Grinza, but tradition deemed it bad luck for the bride and groom to see each other on their wedding day, prior to the ceremony. He decided to take a walk and make sure that the new cabin they would move into was ready.

EARLY THAT SAME MORNING GRINZA SAT UP IN BED, not yet fully awake and coming out of what she first thought was a dream. Then she remembered Noah's threats the night before and knew they were real – knew she had not been dreaming. But, in spite of all that, she vowed not to let it spoil her wedding day.

She continued to sit there for a few minutes, and hearing activity in the kitchen, she arose and joined her mom and dad just as breakfast was being served. "Good morning." her dad greeted her, adding, "Did you sleep well?" "Not really," answered Grinza, to which her mother replied, "I don't think any of us did. Let's have breakfast and talk about the day.

Over the meal they discussed the things they needed to get done before leaving for the church. The wedding ceremony was scheduled for 6:00pm and they planned to get to the church an hour before that to make sure everything was in place.

AS PLANNED, THE LOVELLS ARRIVED AT THE CHURCH at exactly 5 o'clock. Grinza was escorted into a room where she would remain until the ceremony began, with several friends, including Angelica, assigned to stay with her so she wouldn't be alone. Her parents, meanwhile, met with the priest, checked the number of chairs for the people attending to make sure everyone would have a seat, and attended to all the little details that would make the event just perfect.

By 5:30pm, the guests began to arrive, and when Clopin and his parents got there, they were able to welcome everyone and thank them for coming. All that remained was for the rest of the guests to arrive and the wedding ceremony to begin.

AT SIX PM SHARP THE WEDDING PRO-CESSION BEGAN. First down the aisle came the bridesmaids, each accompanied by a groomsman. Next were the Best Man and the Matron of Honor, followed by the Groom and his father, and lastly the Bride herself. As the music to the bridal march began, all eyes were on Grinza. She looked so beautiful dressed in a traditional white gown and her face covered with a veil.

She walked slowly, finally reaching the riser and stepping up on it to join her groom and her parents along with Patrick and Lina Bogdan , whom Grinza and Clopin had selected to act as their wedding godparents.

Shortly into the ceremony their wedding god-parents performed the ritual of *crowning* upon the bride and groom, by placing ceremonial crowns on their heads as symbols declaring them to be the King and Queen of their newly created family.

Grinza remained in a daze throughout the cere-mony, remembering only the crowning, taking her wedding vows and being pronounced "man and wife". How they left the church and got to the reception was a total blur.

THE RECEPTION HALL WAS DECORATED BEAUTIFULLY with flowers at each table and a dance floor set up in front the band. Everyone was eating, drinking and dancing. As Grinza and Clopin visited each table to say hello, most of the guests handed them an envelope containing their wedding gifts, which Grinza gave to Danior to hold for them.

One special table had been reserved for the Guru Sylvanus, Auntie Anselina, and the Bogdans, all very special people to Grinza and Clopin.

About an hour into the reception, a number of her friends escorted Grinza away from the reception hall, out of the building and on to a local pub. This was the traditional "kidnapping" that was part of most gypsy weddings. At the pub they all had a few drinks and sent someone to tell Clopin where they were, and that if he wanted Grinza back he would have to pay the ransom, which in this case, was to pay the bill for the drinks they had at the pub.

When they returned to the reception, their wedding Godmother removed Grinza's veil and replaced it with a pretty scarf. This act symbolized that Grinza was no longer a bride, she was now officially a "wife".

Although the reception would continue all night long and on into the morning, Grinza and Clopin soon left to begin their lives together as husband and wife.

Later that night, when they were alone, Grinza told Clopin what had happened the night before. "I'm really frightened by him", she said about Noah. "I think he really hates us." Remembering how Noah had worn the black scarf the night they announced their engagement, Clopin put his arms around Grinza and swore that he would never let Noah harm her.

ONE DAY SHORTLY AFTER THE WEDDING, Grinza and Clopin were invited to dinner at Clopin's parent's home. They had a wonderful evening reminiscing about the wedding and about some of the guests who drank too much vodka and had to be helped home the next morning. They talked about the "kidnapping" and how much fun that had been. And after a last glass of wine, they left for home.

When they stepped up to their porch, they could see that the front door was slightly ajar. Clopin was sure he had locked it when they left and told Grinza to stay outside while he went in and checked to be sure that no one was there.

In just a few minutes he came back to the door and told Grinza that there was no one there and the house didn't really seem disturbed. "Maybe I did leave the door open." he thought to himself. A little while later they kissed each other good night and went to sleep, thinking nothing more of it.

The next day, while Grinza was ironing clothes and hanging them in the closet, she noticed that the crowns they had been given at the wedding, symbolizing them as the King and Queen of their home, were no longer on the top shelf where she had placed them. That's when she looked down and saw hers lying on the closet floor, but Clopin's was missing. "Strange," she thought, and began looking all over the cabin for it. When she couldn't find it anywhere, she asked Clopin if he had moved it, but he said he hadn't. At that point it became clear to them that Clopin hadn't left the door open the night before – someone had broken into their home and taken Clopin's crown. It didn't even make any sense. Why would anyone want that crown? It had no real value.

Another time they came home to find that someone had thrown raw eggs at the front door and made a mess that took them over an hour to clean up. Who would do something like this? And why? They had no idea.

NOAH HEARNE WATCHED GRINZA AND CLOPIN from a distance as they cleaned up the remains of the eggs he had thrown against their front door. He had still not gotten over being turned down by Grinza only to have her choose someone else shortly after that. Clopin didn't deserve her. And if he had anything to say about it, they would never be happy together.

THAT WINTER, AS CLOPIN WAS WALKING HOME FROM WORK one evening, Noah Hearne stepped out from behind a tree. Before Clopin could react at all, Noah whacked him in the head with a large piece of wood and pushed him to the ground. "I hate you." He yelled and started to kick Clopin in his side. After a few kicks, Clopin felt a severe pain in his ribs on his left side and curled into a ball to stop Noah from kicking him again in the same spot. Noah prepared to kick him again, but suddenly turned and ran away as they both heard someone approaching. It was Angelica Vladua, Grinza's closest friend.

She went to Clopin, still in a ball on the ground, and helped him up. "I can't believe Noah did this," she told him, "but I'm not surprised he wanted to hurt you. Grinza has told me about the threats he has made, but to physically attack you – I just can't believe even he would do that."

Angelica helped Clopin get home and together they told Grinza what had happened. They all agreed that they had to report this to the local constable.

The next morning the three of them went to Constable Jack's office and reported the assault.

Jack told them, "If you will press charges, I'll go arrest him right now."

After his arrest, Noah was charged with two counts – assault, and because he had used a lethal weapon, he was also charged with attempted murder, for which he was eventually convicted and sentenced to jail for 15 – 20 years.

THE NEXT FEW YEARS WENT BY SWIFTLY. Clopin's dream of a furniture business had become a reality. He loved what he was doing, his business was a success and he was able to provide Grinza with a comfortable life. Grinza kept herself busy tending to the cabin, learning to cook Clopin's favorite meals and caring for her cherry tree. When the cherries were ripe, she would pick them, always giving some to her friends and neighbors, and making some into marmalade for the winter months. They often had their parents over for dinner or went to visit them. They were very happy, their lives were good, and they began to think that the time was right for them to have a baby.

ONCE THEY DECIDED TO START A FAMILY, and because Grinza and Clopin were both hoping that they might have a boy, they decided to ask Auntie Anselina if there was any way to make that happen.

"Your chances for having a boy will be greatly increased if you follow this advice," she told them.

"At your most fertile time of the month, place one red rose in a vase on a table. Then light a red candle, which is symbolic of Mars, ruler of vigor and vitality. Next, on a bay leaf – because bay is ruled by the sun – write the phrase 'I wish to conceive a son.' And finally, place the leaf face up next to the candle."

And that is what they did, convinced that their first child would be a son. And the next morning, as she sat under her cherry tree, Grinza shared her joy, confiding in it, whispering "We're going to have a child - a little boy!"

ON GRINZA'S 21ST BIRTHDAY she found out that she was two months pregnant. Clopin had already left for work and she couldn't wait for him to get home so she could share the good news.

When he arrived at the cabin that evening, he could smell the aroma of his favorite meal, pheasant, cooking in the oven. The table was set with a white tablecloth and two candles. Grinza welcomed him with a kiss and a grin on her face that he had come to know meant that she had something special to tell him. He washed up, changed his clothes and came back to the kitchen, sitting down at the table while Grinza poured them each a glass of wine.

Grinza raised her glass to make a toast, saying, "Clopin, I have the most wonderful news. Our prayers have been answered. I am so excited. This morning I learned that I am pregnant! Imagine. I am carrying our first child!"

Hearing this, Clopin raised his glass and clinked it to Grinza's. He was overcome with emotion and couldn't get any words out for a moment. Finally, he blurted, "I am thrilled. You have just made me the happiest man in the world." And he got up from his chair, reached out for Grinza to stand, wrapped his arms around her, and with tears in his eyes he told her he loved her.

ALTHOUGH IT WAS SEVEN MORE MONTHS before the child was due, almost immediately Clopin was at work building a crib for the baby and a rocking chair for Grinza. The idea of being parents was exciting and they spent many hours talking about it. Both Grinza's and Clopin's parents were thrilled. Becoming grandparents was something they had hoped for ever since the wedding.

As the pregnancy progressed, Grinza's stomach began to swell and she was gaining a lot of weight. She often found herself tired after the least exertion. Cleaning and cooking became more and more difficult, so Clopin would help out with both. He was indefatigable, going to work early each morning, coming home and washing clothes or making dinner and doing the dishes.

The baby was due in April and by March Grinza longed for the day when she would get her figure and her old energy back. She could no longer go for long walks or even take care of her cherry tree, so Clopin had also taken over that responsibility.

ON THE MORNING OF APRIL 7TH, IN THE YEAR 1911, Grinza awoke feeling a wetness in her bed and thought she had wet it in her sleep, but when she sat up, she realized that this was different. Her waters had broken, and she ran to the bathroom to clean herself up. She was glad that Clopin had not yet left for work and, almost in a panic, she let him know that the baby was coming. There was a lady, Dena Petrescu who lived just down the street and had helped deliver most of the babies in their neighborhood, and she asked Clopin to run and get her.

In a few minutes Clopin brought Dena to the cabin and she had Grinza lay down on the bed so she could examine her. "Yes, the baby is near," she said. Then she asked Clopin to bring clean sheets and towels, and to boil water. "You just lay here and try to stay still for now," she told Grinza. "The contractions are still far enough apart that we have a little while."

Hearing that, Clopin told Grinza that he was going to let their parents know what was happening, and he left, returning as soon as he had told them. He let Grinza know that they would all be coming there shortly.

IT DIDN'T TAKE LONG BEFORE IT WAS TIME. Dena knew exactly what to do and coached Grinza on her breathing and pushing. It was a fairly quick delivery, which was unusual for a first child. "Congratulations," said Dena. "You have a brand new, beautiful baby girl!"

Hearing that, they were shocked! All this time they had been convinced they were having a baby boy. And while they were indeed shocked, they were not in the least disappointed. They were thrilled. As Dena handed the baby to Grinza, Clopin ran to her, looked at the baby and started crying. "She's absolutely beautiful!" he shouted. And, he leaned over and gave, first Grinza, then the baby, a kiss.

They had a baby now, but not a name for her. They had been so sure they were having a boy that they hadn't even considered any girls names.

"Let's name her Cura, after your mom," said Clopin. And Grinza agreed. And her mom was honored and thrilled about that.

Gypsies believe that a baby born on a full moon is lucky and will have a charmed life. Although baby Cura was born in the morning, there was indeed a full moon that night, and all agreed that she would be forever charmed. And to this child, they divined the gifts of *seer* (visionary) and wisdom.

Grinza couldn't wait to share her great news with her best friend, Angelica and with her cherry tree.

TWO YEARS LATER GRINZA AND CLOPIN were again blessed with another child. This time they had the little boy that they so fervently believed they were going to have the first time. They called him Nelson. And, two years after that, when they were blessed with a child for the third time, their family was complete. There was Grinza, Clopin, Cura, Nelson and the new baby, their second boy, Patin.

During the summer of 1915, their daughter Cura was four years old. One day she came home from playing in the sun and she looked very different. She had broken out in freckles! Grinza, who had so detested her own at one time in her life, absolutely loved Cura's. "You are so beautiful." she told her. "I love your freckles! Now you are just like your *dai* (mommy)."

FIVE YEARS WENT BY. It was 1920 and the children, now 9, 7 and 5 years old all did well in school. Cura, the eldest, often helped her mom with the cooking and cleaning. She also helped take care of the cherry tree and really enjoyed harvesting its cherries and giving them out to family and friends.

Nelson, the first-born son and now seven years old, was a natural athlete. He was a very good swimmer and was the fastest runner in his grade. His younger brother Patin looked up to his older brother and tried to be just like him. Clopin's furniture business prospered and together, the Rosu family was well liked and well respected in the village.

Each year the village held a New Year's Eve party in the square. This party was attended by almost everyone. The festivities began in the afternoon and continued well on into the night. Afternoon activities included food and events for the whole family: three-legged races, relay races, and father-son horse racing where both rode together on the same horse and raced against other father-son teams. There were also mother-daughter cake and pie baking contests. This was a family affair, and everyone looked forward to it.

Everyone had hopes and dreams for the coming year. Clopin hoped his business would be good enough that he could afford an apprentice to help him. And Grinza hoped that this might be the year they could afford to start her cherry orchard.

CHAPTER SEVEN

AUNTIE ANSELINA'S BEQUEST

EARLY IN 1921 the entire village was shocked to hear that Auntie Anselina had quietly passed away in her sleep. The very next day the Guru Sylvanus made a rare appearance in the village. His first stop was at Grinza and Clopin's home. "It is so sad," he told them. We will all miss Auntie Anselina very much."

Grinza stared at him for a second, unable to say anything. Finally, she pulled herself together. "Yes, it is so sad," she agreed in a whisper. Then added, as tears filled her eyes, "She had always been so special to me."

Sylvanus continued, "You are my first stop this morning because that was Auntie Anselina's request. To visit Grinza first and to give her a very special gift, which I've brought with me."

Again, Grinza didn't know what to say. "Something for me?"

"Yes," said Sylvanus, "she wanted you to have this." And with that, he handed her a small velvet box that she opened and gasped, "Oh my god. I can't believe she left this to me. I have always admired this beautiful ring."

To which Sylvanus responded, "She told me that if you hadn't saved her, she wouldn't have it any longer. It would have been stolen by that horrible man in the woods. And so, when it could no longer be hers, she wanted you to have it. She hoped it would make a difference in your life and bring you great joy."

"I don't know what to say. I have such special, wonderful memories of her."

Then the Guru Sylvanus left to notify the rest of the village about Auntie Anselina's passing.

THAT NIGHT GRINZA DREAMED ABOUT AUNTIE ANSELINA. And in her dream, Auntie Anselina came to her and told her that she wished she could have left her more, but the only thing of value she owned, was her ring. And she went on to say that she wanted her to use that ring to bring about her own greatest dreams. She said that if she could help Grinza get what she dreamed of, she would deem it an honor and a credit to her own life and her memory.

The next day Grinza shared her dream with Clopin. "You know how much I loved Auntie Anselina," she told him. "In this dream, she came to me and told me she wanted me to use the ring to fulfill my dreams. To sell it and use the money anyway I wanted. As much as I would love to keep it as a memory of her, if we can sell it and use the money to start a cherry orchard, that orchard would be a living tribute to her and as much a memory of her as the ring itself."

ROMANIA HAS ALWAYS BEEN ONE OF THE TOP PRODUCERS of cherries in the world, and Romanian cherries were among the best and most sought after produced anywhere.

The first obstacle Grinza and Clopin faced in starting a cherry orchard, was to find the land and acquire it. They wanted twenty acres and there was only one field that size for sale. The owner was asking $80 an acre.

Their total startup costs including the land at $80.00 per acre, would be $3,950 plus the costs of picking and packing. Now they had to find out if the ring was worth that much.

Clopin went to the wealthiest man in the village and asked if he would like to buy the beautiful emerald ring. The man knew it was the most beautiful ring in the village and he did want it. "How much do you want for it? he asked Clopin.

When Clopin told him he would sell it for $4,000, the man shook his head 'No' and said he would only pay half that.

Clopin had an idea. He knew they needed $4,000 to pay for the land and plant the twenty acres with trees; but, he thought, what if we buy all the land but only plant five acres each year. It would take four years until they had the full orchard planted, but their startup, first year costs would be less. He could do that with $2,200,

"Half is not enough he told the man, "but I can sell the ring for $2,500. That is the lowest I can go."

The man agreed to the price and gave Clopin the $2,500.

GRINZA WAS CLEANING THE CABIN when Clopin's mother, Natalia, knocked on her door. When she opened the door to let her in, the look on her face told Grinza that something was wrong. "What is it?" she asked.

"It is Elijah," She burst into tears. "He was chopping wood and slipped. The axe cut his leg deeply and he lost a great deal of blood. He is in bed now, but I am very frightened."

Natalia fell into Grinza's outstretched arms and they stood there holding each other, both crying.

"Who is with him?" Grinza asked, knowing that a seriously ill or dying gypsy is never supposed to be left alone.

"My neighbor is staying with him until I get back. Grinza, I am so frightened. I don't think he is going to make it. I have to tell Clopin. He needs to be there."

CLOPIN WAS SO EXCITED ABOUT SELL-ING THE RING. He ran home to tell Grinza the good news. She would finally have her cherry orchard.

When he arrived at the cabin, he saw his mother and Grinza hugging. He saw that they were both crying, and he became frightened. "Mother, what are you doing here? What's wrong?" he cried out.

"Oh, Clopin," she said, "It's *Dadus*. He had a very bad accident. We need to be with him."

Clopin hugged his mom and with tears in his eyes, he took his mother's hand and led her back to her home. All thoughts of his good news were gone.

Grinza left her cabin and went to find her mom whose house was nearby. Both Cura and Danior were home when she got there. She told them the terrible news and together they left for the Rosu's home.

By the time they arrived, Elijah had passed. Natalia and Clopin were gathering his few possessions to begin the tradition of burning them, leaving only his best suit in which to be buried. Valuables were to be kept or given away, but clothing and other possessions had to be burned.

Candles were lit around the bed on which he was lying, to light the way to the afterlife.

The funeral was held the next day. Natalia, Clopin, Grinza and all the family members dressed in white, representing purity. Villagers lined the streets as the funeral procession passed their homes on the way to the cemetery.

Clopin and Grinza didn't want Natalia to have to live alone and offered to have her come live with them. It would be good for her and good for their children to be around their grandmother every day. And so, the day after the funeral Natalia moved in with them.

CLOPIN PURCHASED THE TWENTY ACRES for the orchard and together, he and Grinza planned how they would proceed.

The land was open to the main road that ran through the village and this would be good for getting the cherries to market, but to help secure the orchard, Clopin built a six-foot fence around the entire property. The only access was through the gate which he built wide enough to get large trucks in and out. With a padlock on the gate, Clopin felt the orchard would be secure enough to keep out anyone who might want to steal their equipment or even their cherries.

That evening Clopin gathered his family around him and let them know that the orchard was finally ready and that in a few months they would begin planting the first five acres. He told them that they would each have a role in the planting and how special it was that it would be a wonderful family run orchard. He reminded them that this was Grinza's dream and that they would all be a part of making it a reality.

Grinza looked at her family proudly and said a silent prayer that all would go as planned.

DURING THE NEXT SPRING, IN 1923, the Rosu family planted five acres, as planned. After paying $1,600 for the land and almost $600 for the trees, they had used up almost all the money they had received for Auntie Anselina's ring. Now they had to try and save up another $600 each year for three more years, in order to plant the rest of the twenty acres, five acres at a time.

In 1923 Cura was twelve, Nelson was ten and Patin, eight. Each was old enough and anxious to help out in the orchard.

They began the planting in June, when school was out. After breakfast each day, Clopin would leave for his workshop, and Grinza, along with the three children, went to the orchard. There they unloaded the wagons, dug holes in the ground, and planted the trees in them. It was dirty work, and it was hard, but no one seemed to mind. They often sang songs while they worked.

At eight years old, Patin was the first to get tired each day and often sat down to rest. Grinza packed water, juice and sandwiches for lunch and they ate sitting at a small table that Clopin had built for them. After lunch they always played games before getting back to work. It was a good life filled with hard work and fun. And working together as a family, strengthened the closeness they felt for each other. Clopin saw this and was happy about it, but a little jealous that he couldn't join them each day and be part of it.

Of the three children, Nelson was the most popular. He loved sports and made friends easily. Cura was the shyest and tried not to be in the limelight. Patin looked up to his brother Nelson and wanted to be just like him.

One time the three of them convinced their parents that they were old enough to go camping and spend the night on the outskirts of the village in a tent, by a lake.

Early the morning of their adventure, Grinza made them sandwiches and sent them on their way with the tent, the sandwiches and a few bottles of water. They also carried fishing poles, blankets to sleep on and a few other supplies. Grinza stood in front of the house and watched them trek up the nearby hill as her eyes filled with tears and she realized that her children were growing up.

When they arrived at the campground, by the edge of the lake, they decided to put up the tent before doing anything else. Cura unfolded the canvas, while Nelson and Patin pounded stakes into the ground so they could tie the tent down.

While they were putting up the tent, Patin noticed a large dog watching them from a distance. Knowing that packs of stray dogs were commonplace outside the village, and that they could be dangerous, he told Cura and Nelson. The three of them armed themselves with sticks and continued putting up the tent. "As long as it doesn't get any closer and we don't see any others, we're fine," Nelson told them.

"We just have to keep an eye on it."

When they finally had the tent up, they stored their food and supplies inside it. It was starting to get cool by then, so Nelson asked Cura to gather some small tree branches while he tried to start a fire.

Then Nelson asked Patin to stay and watch the fire while he and Cura went to the lake to catch some fish for dinner.

They left, carrying their fishing poles and Patin sat close to the fire, singing to himself. Breathing in the outdoor air and smelling the fire, Patin was invigorated. He loved his brother and sister and was really happy being with them. And, being by themselves, without their parents, he also felt pretty darn grown up.

Remembering the dog, Patin looked over to the spot he last saw it, but it wasn't there. Looking carefully around he found it much closer to the tent and fire, but still alone. The dog stood perfectly still, watching Patin, then slowly started to approach him, its tail wagging. Patin wasn't sure what to do, but when the dog came all the way to him, he reached out his hand and patted the top of its head.

"Good boy," Patin told him, and the dog sat down, next to Patin and laid its head in his lap. "He is beautiful," thought Patin, "Large and powerful, yet somehow gentle." Patin again stroked the dog's head and it nuzzled up against him. And Patin sensed that this would be his dog and his best friend forever.

At the lake, Cura had just caught two fish. So far, Nelson hadn't caught any. "Guess girls are just better fishermen than boys," she teased him. And they both laughed a few minutes later when she caught yet another. "Guess we have enough for dinner." She told Nelson, and they picked up the fish and their gear and started walking back to the campground. As they approached the tent, they saw that the fire was still going, but they found Patin fast asleep with that stray dog lying beside him.

"I think Patin found a new friend," Cura whispered, so she wouldn't wake them up. "Think *dai* will let him keep it?" "I think so," replied Nelson, also whispering, "We'll soon find out."

That evening when they ate, Patin gave some of his fish to the dog, which he decided to name *Decebal*, a Romanian name meaning 'One who is strong and powerful'. But Patin soon found Decebal too long a name and shortened it to 'Deba'.

The next morning, the three of them, along with Deba, left the camp and walked home. When they arrived at the house, Cura and Nelson went in and Patin remained in the yard with Deba.

Grinza was so glad to see them. She wouldn't admit it, but secretly she had been worried that something would happen to them. Giving them each a hug she asked,

"Where is Patin?" And they told her about the dog and how much Patin wanted to keep it as his own. "Please *dai*," begged Cura, "let him keep the dog. A pet will be good for him." And Grinza agreed.

The very next day Clopin build a large doghouse with the name 'Deba' on the wood panel over the doorway. And the family had grown by one more.

THREE MORE YEARS WENT BY and the whole twenty acres had been planted. It had been four years since they had started the orchard and those original five acres now began producing cherries. This was a time to celebrate, and they decided to have a grand opening the day before they began picking those five acres.

Invitations were sent to the entire village. Even the Guru Sylvanus promised to be there. In a few years, when all twenty acres were producing cherries, Grinza's Orchard would be the largest business in the village and employ the most people.

The official opening was an exciting moment for everyone. When all had gathered in a clearing just inside the gate, vodka was poured, and Sylvanus stood atop a small box to make a toast.

"Raise your glasses, all." He started. "This is a monumental occasion for our village. It is symbolic of our future – the beginning of a new prosperity in which we will all share." "So, here's to Grinza and Clopin, who have worked so hard to make their dream come true, and in doing so, have contributed so much to the rest of us." Grinza, Clopin, we are so proud of you!" And with that, the drinking and dancing and celebrating began and continued on late into the night.

THE WHOLE FAMILY CONTINUED TO WORK THE ORCHARD every day, and Patin always brought Deba along with him.

Because it was only the first five acres that bore fruit, Grinza and her children, now aged 15, 13 and 11, were able to handle the harvest themselves. They picked cherries day after day, filling their buckets and emptying them into the twenty-pound boxes, getting them ready to be shipped. When all 235 trees were picked clean, they had produced almost 7,000 pounds of cherries! And they knew they would turn a nice profit.

To celebrate they held a party for their friends and neighbors. The entire village was proud of them and what they had accomplished. And when they saw the boxes of cherries, stamped with the words *"Grinza's Orchard, Cojasca Village, Romania"* they were proud that the cherries carried their village name and that its name would be seen all across the country.

IN 1927, WITH TEN ACRES PRODUCING FRUIT, and with the income from Clopin's furniture business still growing, the Rosu's were becoming one of the wealthier families in the village. Because they could no longer do all the work themselves, they were also becoming one of the major employers, with fifteen people hired to maintain and harvest their crop.

Their older daughter, Cura, turned sixteen that year, and several local young men had noticed the beautiful young woman she had become.

"You are such a beautiful girl, Cura," Grinza told her. "You will soon have many suitors. You must be careful in selecting the man with whom you will spend the rest of your life. He must be a good man, a kind and generous man. A hard worker. A man like your father. And only such a man will we approve."

One day that year, Clopin came home and called Grinza aside. "I have bad news," he whispered, "Noah Hearne has been released from prison. He is back in the village and saying bad things about us. We have to let the children know that they must be careful. He is a bad man."

Shortly after that, Grinza arrived at the orchard one morning to find that the padlock on the gate had been tampered with. It was still locked, but someone had obviously tried to open it. "Noah," she thought.

That night she told Clopin about the padlock, and they agreed that the orchard had to be even more secure. And so, they decided to hire a guard to watch the gate at night so they wouldn't have to worry.

BY 1929 ALL TWENTY ACRES OF THE ORCHARD were mature and producing cherries. Clopin, Grinza and their family were doing quite well and enjoying the fruits of their labor. Clopin hired some local villagers and together they built a large addition onto their home, which was now too large to call a cabin any longer – it was, indeed, a large and comfortable house. A home for their family.

Everything was going well for them... until October 24th when the great stock market crash sent the economy, worldwide, into a tumble. Most currencies lost value, and people's savings couldn't buy nearly as much as previously. Everyone had less money and many people began to have trouble paying for even the necessities. And while food was a necessity, expensive cherries were not. The price for cherries fell to a twenty-year low and those with cherry orchards were hit very hard. The cost of producing the cherries stayed the same, but the amount of money the cherries brought on the market, was much less than before. And for Grinza and Clopin, it was a double whammy. Much of Clopin's furniture sat in his warehouse, People who had ordered from him no longer had the money to pay for it. Fortunately, Grinza and Clopin had some savings, but how long they would last, they really didn't know.

The entire investment and banking world was in a frenzy. Some people in America who had lost their life savings, committed suicide by jumping off the roofs of fifty story buildings.

In the village of Cojasca, life went on pretty much as usual, but a few of the wealthier families, like the Rosus, had to let their employees go, so the financial crisis was felt by everyone.

THE WINTER OF 1929 WAS ANOTHER SEVERELY COLD ONE. Food and wood for fireplaces was hard to find and expensive. In many ways it was reminiscent of the winter of 1906 when Grinza had chopped down her beloved cherry tree to save her family.

Grinza and Clopin had two fireplaces in their home, but could only keep one going, so the whole family had to sleep in the living room, some on the floor, others on chairs and on a couch. They did bring a bed in to the living room for Clopin's mom, Natalia, who was much older than the rest.

The cherry orchard was alright because it was always barren in the winter, so no crops were ruined.

Everyone in the village helped each other out, sharing firewood and food with those less fortunate. So, somehow, the Rosu family and the rest of the village managed to survive.

On November 13th the stock market began to slowly turn around and the investment brokers were once again becoming optimistic.

By March the ground had begun to thaw, and

everyone knew that spring was just around the corner. Now it was time to get the orchard ready. Everyone in the Rosu family helped. Leaves were raked, branches cleared of any remaining ice or snow, and the ground cleared of any other debris that had gathered during the winter.

By April, small buds could be seen on some of the branches. By May there was a beautiful crop of cherries as far as the eye could see across the twenty-acre orchard. Grinza was so proud of all they had accomplished. Out of her love for her very first cherry tree, given to her by her parents, had grown this magnificent orchard. Out of dreams she had built a reality.

GRINZA'S
DREAMS ABLAZE

CHAPTER EIGHT

THE DREAM GOES UP IN SMOKE

BY JUNE THE CROP WAS READY TO HAR-VEST. Using the last of their savings, Grinza hired enough villagers to pick and pack the cherries. Although the price she would get for them was a bit lower than last season, there would still be some profit. And as the world came out of the economic crash, she hoped the price of cherries would soon be rising.

They were planning to pick the cherries beginning the second week in June; however, on June seventh when Grinza went into the kitchen to prepare breakfast, she looked out the window and saw black smoke and fire off in the distance. The smoke billowed high into the sky and the flames were shooting straight up.

She woke Clopin and together they ran outside in their pajamas to see if they could tell what was burning. By this time many of the villagers were out on the road leading to their orchard and shouting, "The orchard is on fire! The orchard is burning!" Grinza and Clopin ran back into their home, woke everyone and changed into their clothes, running out of the house and down the road to the orchard. Their children, along with Clopin's mother, Natalia, followed closely on their heels.

As they approached the wall enclosing the orchard, they could see the tops of the trees. They were all on fire. The gate to the orchard stood wide open. How could this be? Just when things were beginning to look better, the entire orchard was going up in flames. The guard they had hired lay on the dirt path in front of the gate, unconscious. He had been hit over the head with a wooden club that lay beside him.

Nothing could be done. The orchard was too far gone to save it. The whole family stood there in silence, tears streaming from their faces. All their hard work, all their sacrifices over the years, all gone in one moment. Grinza slowly sank to her knees, her hands covering her face, a wail escaping her lips. They were all devastated.

They stayed there along with many of the villagers, until the fire burned itself out. By then the ground was black with ashes. Here and there small embers flared up and then extinguished themselves.

By this time the guard had revived and was sitting up. Fortunately, he seemed alright, but he had not seen the man who had hit him.

And then, everyone left in a daze. Grinza and Clopin walked back home, hand in hand, without saying a word to each other. Each deep in their own thoughts.

None of them could fall asleep in the Rosu house that night. No one knew what was going to happen to them. Clopin's furniture business was picking up, so they had money coming in. But everything Grinza had dreamed of, had striven for, was lost. Auntie Anselina's ring had been sold and it had all come to naught.

The next morning, as the sun came up, Grinza and Clopin walked back to the orchard. On the way they stopped at Grinza's only remaining cherry tree – the one in the front yard of the first cabin in which she had ever lived – the one the Guru Sylvanus had divined her. And Grinza cried as she told her tree about the orchard.

When they got to the orchard, the gate was still wide open. Up ahead they saw Patin and his dog Deba digging through some ash strewn on the ground along the main path that wove through the orchard. Looking at the devastation, Grinza started to cry but stopped short when she heard Patin yell out, "*Dadus, Dai* - look at this!"

Grinza and Clopin ran over to Patin and were startled as they noticed several red gasoline cans that Deba had uncovered in the ashes. "What is that? How did they get here?" she asked Clopin. Then the two of them simultaneously mouthed the words, "Noah Hearne!"

Immediately, all of them – Grinza, Clopin, Patin and his dog Deba, went to the constable. Clopin told him about the gasoline cans and Noah's threats. And based on that, an investigation was opened to find out how this devasting fire that affected the entire village, had been started.

NOAH SAT ON HIS FRONT PORCH AND WATCHED THE FLAMES as they rose from the orchard. "What do you think of him now," he thought, "Bet you're sorry you married Clopin, aren't you?"

CONSTABLE JACK STARTED HIS INVESTI-GATION with a search around the still smoldering orchard property. He took pictures of the gas cans. He took pictures of the gate lock which had been smashed open. And he found a large hammer near the gate that was almost certainly used to smash it. This particular hammer had a handle that was wrapped in black tape to help with the grip.

First, he interviewed the guard who couldn't give him any more information Next he interviewed many of the villagers to see if anyone had seen anything unusual the night the fire began. Two brothers out for a walk that night said that they passed Noah on the road that led to the orchard, but they were about a quarter of a mile from the orchard when they passed him, so they couldn't say for sure if he even went there.

The interviews took Constable Jack a few days, and finally he went to see Noah, who he found sitting in his front yard, drinking a can of beer. He asked Noah where he had been that night and Noah responded that he had been home all night, never leaving his house.

"Funny about that," said Constable Jack. "Two eyewitnesses put you near the orchard just before the fire broke out." Then Constable Jack asked Noah to show him his barn.

In the barn Jack found two more gasoline cans that were identical to the ones he had taken the pictures of, and a set of tools, all with handles wrapped in black tape.

"Noah Hearne," said Jack, "I'm arresting you for arson – for starting the fire that burned down *Grinza's Orchard*." And then he handcuffed Noah and led him to the jail.

Word of Noah's arrest spread quickly throughout the village. For most of the people it was no surprise. They knew what kind of man he was, and they knew he had threatened Clopin.

For Grinza and Clopin the arrest didn't settle anything. Their orchard was destroyed and there was no way they could ever put together the money it would take to reopen it. Knowing how much Grinza loved the orchard, for Clopin it was the saddest day of his life. For Grinza it was the end of a dream.

CHAPTER NINE

CLOPIN'S GIFT TO GRINZA

THROUGH THE FALL AND WINTER OF 1930, the orchard remained untouched. It just sat there - an ash encrusted, barren, twenty acres of land. Grinza somehow managed to go about her day-to-day life but with no real enthusiasm, even on birthdays and holidays.

Clopin went to work each day, but worried about Grinza. His business was flourishing but he too, had lost his enthusiasm, his zest for life. All of that had gone down in flames in one night that June. Clopin wondered how he could help his family, but the loss of the orchard weighed too heavily on all of them.

He just didn't know what to do. Then, one day, as he was completing the final sanding on a kitchen table he was making, he had an idea. An idea that he would have to keep secret for the time being.

CLOPIN'S DREAM HAD ALWAYS BEEN to have his own furniture business. And now he had it. And it was more successful than he ever thought it might be. He had achieved and surpassed all his dreams. Life had been so good to him. He had his business, he had his family, he was well respected in the village. But Grinza's despondence since the loss of her orchard weighed heavily on him. He could never be happy if Grinza wasn't. And he was prepared to sacrifice anything to change that.

One day in March of 1931, Clopin told Grinza that he had a surprise for her. He blindfolded her and led her to her cherry tree, where he sat her down on a blanket. Sitting down next to her, he removed her blindfold. "Clopin," she cried out, "why did you bring me here?" "Because," he answered, "because it is in this exact spot that some of the most wonderful moments in your life have taken place."

He then unrolled and spread out before her, a long paper with words written on it. Grinza looked at the paper, saw the words, **"GRINZA'S ORCHARD"** on it and was stunned. "What is this?" she asked. "What does this mean?"

"It means," he told her, "that we are going to rebuild your –"

"You know we can't do that," she interrupted. We'll never have enough money to reopen the orchard." To which he replied, "I have the money and I have already hired a crew to clean out the land. And I have already ordered the trees. Before this summer is over, we will be fully planted. And because the trees I have ordered are mature, we will have the full twenty acres producing fruit next year."

"Clopin, what is going on? That would take a fortune – a fortune we do not have."

"Oh, but we do," he answered. I sold the furniture business and we have enough money to do this."

"In fact," he went on to say, "it is already done. *Grinza's Orchard* is once again open for business."

GRINZA KNEW HOW MUCH CLOPIN'S FURNITURE BUSINESS meant to him. She knew it had always been his dream, much as the orchard had been hers. For him to give up his dream in order to give her hers, was the ultimate gift of love. Through this sacrifice, his love for her was the most beautiful gift she could imagine. She turned to Clopin and wrapped her arms around him. Through tears she couldn't stop, Grinza let him know that she loved him with all her heart and soul. And the shade of the cherry tree under which they now sat, was once again the source of so much happiness in her life.

GRINZA WAS NOW FORTY-ONE YEARS OLD. Their daughter Cura was twenty, their oldest son, Nelson was eighteen and the youngest, Patin, was sixteen. All of them grown up. All still living at home, but both Grinza and Clopin realized that they would soon want to move out and be on their own. Patin and Nelson wanted to continue working at the orchard. They loved the work and they loved being part of the family business. Cura helped out there too but was showing interest in a young man from the village and might soon have marriage in mind.

That year, Grinza's parents, Cura and Danior, both passed away. They were in their sixties, which was considered old then, and died of natural causes. Danior went first, and Cura followed just three months later. Their whole family was sad as they said goodbye to them at their funerals. They had all been such a major part of one another's lives, and they would be dearly missed.

SHORTLY AFTER THAT, CLOPIN WAS AP-PROACHED by the young man Cura had been seeing. His name was Pali Young, and he worked as a gardener for a wealthy family in the village. He asked for Clopin's permission to marry his daughter Cura, and Clopin was pleased to say yes.

The next year was a very busy one for the whole family. Cura's wedding and the reopening of the orchard consumed most of their time. Grinza still visited the cherry tree that sat in what had once been her parent's yard. And, they gave that home to Cura and her husband Pali as a wedding gift.

Clopin did miss his woodworking but managed to find time to do some when he wasn't busy with the orchard.

LIVING IN THIS SMALL VILLAGE IN ROMANIA, the Lovells often felt isolated from the rest of the world. They did sell their cherries throughout Romania, but beyond that the rest of the world seemed far removed from their everyday lives. That is, until September 1939 when World War II broke out, and the lives of everyone in Europe changed forever.

To avoid war on their own land, and to avoid having to send troops to fight in another country, the then Romanian King, King Carol II, declared Romania to be a neutral country, meaning that they would not take sides nor participate in any way, in this war.

Unfortunately, political groups such as the Fascist *Iron Guard* gained popularity in Romania and wanted Romania to form an alliance with Nazi Germany.

This led to an uprising ending with a new ruler, *Maresal Ion Antonescu*. And with him in charge, Romania officially joined forces with Germany. As one result, Romanian troops were sent to fight against Russia at the Eastern Front. Only because the Lovells were considered farmers and vital to the food supply of the nation, neither Nelson nor Patin were forced to join the army.

GRINZA TURNED FIFTY YEARS OLD IN 1940. By now life in this small Romanian village had changed with the times. Everyone had electricity. Most everyone had telephones. Evenings were often spent listening to shows that were broadcast on the radio. The village even had a movie theater.

THE YEARS HAD BEEN GOOD TO CLOPIN AND GRINZA. By 1943 they had 2 grandchildren – a boy, seven years old, and a girl, five. Grinza loved spending time with them, babysitting, baking their favorite cookies and just watching them grow up. Her family was her pride and joy.

Their sons had not yet married but they had moved into the village. Nelson was thirty years old and was seeing a young woman who taught school in the village. He had taken over much of the management of the orchard.

Patin was put in charge of the packing and shipping. In addition to his other duties, Nelson oversaw the picking and maintenance. Clopin and Grinza were still active in the business but had stepped back from most of their day-to-day duties. They were mostly involved in the major decisions that had to be made.

Clopin's mom, Natalia, had passed on only three years after Elijah. Their grandchildren now tended to Grinza's cherry tree that still stood proudly in the yard in front of their house.

EVERY SUNDAY GRINZA HAD THE WHOLE FAMILY OVER FOR DINNER. Grinza, Clopin, their two sons, their daughter Cura and her husband and their two children, always arrived around three o'clock. Dinner was served at five pm sharp. Always. It had become a tradition. No one missed out on this Sunday dinner unless they were sick. It was the one day of the week that they all sat down to eat, drink wine and talk about the things going on in their lives. It was Grinza's favorite day of the week.

Grinza volunteered to help others in need whenever she could. She was beloved by most everyone in the village. One time a widow with a young child became quite ill and couldn't take care of her daughter. Grinza volunteered to stay at their home and take care of both the mother and the child for as long as it took to get them back on their feet. She was a fixture in the village, and everyone counted on her to lead the way when any crisis arose.

With more time on her hands now, Grinza took up knitting. She knit dresses for her granddaughter, hats and a vest for her grandson, and blankets and scarves for her children and for Clopin.

BY THE LATE 1940'S, Grinza found herself tiring out more frequently than she ever remembered. She still enjoyed taking long walks, alone, to think about her life and how wonderful it was, but she found that she had to walk slower than she did only a few years earlier. And on these walks, she always stopped to speak to her special cherry tree.

"Life has been so good to me," she told the tree one afternoon on the way home from one of her less and less frequent walks. "I have my family, I have the orchard, I have a wonderful husband and a wonderfully rewarding life… and I have you - the cherry tree that has been such an important part of my life. Always there for me when I needed to talk to you." And with that, she smiled and walked on home, knowing how exceptionally blessed her whole life had been.

IN 1950, GRINZA AND CLOPIN BOTH TURNED SIXTY YEARS OLD. They were considered elders by the villagers and were often called upon for their advice about personal matters and business issues.

Grinza's health was not as good as it could be. She suffered from pains in her legs and shortness of breath when she walked too far, so she didn't go out as much as she once did.

Clopin was now bald with a sparse white beard. Grinza always told him that he looked 'distinguished'. Clopin wasn't so sure.

On September 20th, Grinza's sixtieth birthday, the whole family gathered in Grinza's house to celebrate. Cura baked Grinza's favorite cake – chocolate with vanilla icing and, of course, one of the orchard's own cherries on top.

Grinza was happy to have her whole family together but didn't feel well and shortly after they all sang *Happy Birthday*, she apologized for being tired and had to lay down.

THE VILLAGE MOURNS
A GREAT LOSS

GRINZA CLOPIN

LOVING WIFE
MOTHER
GRANDMOTHER

1890—1950

CHAPTER TEN

THE VILLAGE MOURNS ITS LOSS

ONE DAY, IN THE AFTERNOON, AFTER A LONG WALK, Clopin arrived home to find Grinza lying on the sofa, unable to breath well. He tried to get her to sit up, but she couldn't. He didn't know what to do, so he just tried to keep her comfortable. He sensed this wasn't good but didn't want to believe what was happening. She lay on the couch that night and fell in and out of sleep often. Clopin stayed up the entire night, taking care of her.

When morning came and she was no better, he called Cura, told her what was happening and asked her to get her brothers and come quickly to their home. Then he moved Grinza to their bedroom so she would be more comfortable.

When they arrived, they found Clopin in the bedroom, seated next to the bed, holding Grinza's hand. "Here are the children." they heard him say, and saw their mother turn her head towards them.

Cura was the first to speak. "*Dai,* how are you?" she asked.

"Not so good," her mom wheezed. She tried to smile but couldn't hold back from the pain she was suffering. She reached out her arms and whispered, "Come to me, my children."

As the three of them stepped close to the bed, Grinza touched them one by one and smiled. "You have each brought me so much happiness over the years," she said. "Do not be sad. My time has come, but my life has been wonderful – because of you and your *dadus*.

And then, as if she had been waiting for her children to arrive so she could say goodbye, her body shuddered, and she was gone. "No." shouted Cura. And she reached out to her mother, cradling her face in her hands and kissing her. And one by one each of the others did the same.

Clopin continued to hold Grinza's hand, whispering softly to her. He told her how lucky he had been to have her in his life. He told her how much he loved her and always would, and then he began crying, long loud sobs that broke the children's hearts.

It was October 20, 1950, exactly one month after Grinza had turned sixty years old. With Clopin overcome with grief and barely able to function, Nelson took over for him. True to gypsy tradition, he placed lit candles around the bed on which his mother lay, to light the way to the afterlife.

The next day Clopin spoke to Cura and her husband, Pali, about where he wanted to bury Grinza. "That tree was her most prized and beloved possession, even more so than the orchard."

"Under that tree, where she spent so many hours reflecting on the joys in her life, that's where she should eternally rest." And they agreed.

THE NEXT DAY THE FUNERAL PROCESSION slowly wound its way through the town. Villagers mourned, cried, and even wailed, as the horse and buggy carrying Grinza passed the house in which they had been living, passed Grinza's Orchard and came to a halt in front of the first cabin Grinza had called home. There, under the old cherry tree, Grinza was laid to rest.

Their three children and grandchild were in attendance, as were many friends. These included The Guru Sylvanus – now the oldest living man in the village, Angelica, who had been Grinza's best friend since they were children, Patrick Bogdan whom Grinza had found lying in the grassy woods with a shard of glass in his leg, and his parents, Lina and Gilli Bogdan.

At the end of the funeral ceremony, Clopin walked to the pulpit and spoke.

"DEAR FRIENDS AND RELATIVES," HE BE-
GAN, this is the saddest day of my life. Grinza,
whom I love so dearly, is gone. None of our lives
will ever be the same. She is gone, but she is still
here among us in spirit. I am left with so many
signs of all she was – her orchard, our children, this
cherry tree that she so loved. And how appropri-
ate it is that she be buried here in the very spot
upon which she and I began our life together over
forty-two years ago."

"I have so many wonderful memories of Grinza,
my partner through life. I remember how I first
noticed her in the village and wanted to speak to
her but was too shy to approach her. I remember
hearing about her chopping down her first cherry
tree, the tree she so loved, to keep her sick parents warm during the cold, cold winter of 1906,
and I remember the day Sylvanus gifted her a new
tree, this tree under which we now stand to wish
her goodbye."

"I remember the love and lumps in our hearts
when our first child, Cura, was born. And the sheer
joy she expressed when her orchard first opened,
followed by the intense sorrow when it was burned
to the ground. From the moment she got her first
cherry tree, Grinza had begun dreaming of her own
orchard. Next to her family, she loved her cherry
trees the most."

"Grinza was a strong woman, the finest I ever met and while I loved having her by my side all these years, I shall now endeavor to carry on for her sake, no matter how much I will miss her. God, thank you for the most wonderous gift you have chosen to give me – the gift of Grinza." To which he added to himself, "Goodnight my beloved."

And the entire village went to sleep that night with a sadness and with a tear in their eyes, but also with a sense of comfort in knowing how much Grinza had added to their own lives.

And, in her honor, over the next few months, many villagers planted cherry trees in their own yards.

Epilogue

For the next year, life had gone on normally for Clopin and the children.

The Orchard's business was growing by leaps and bounds. It was rapidly becoming one of the most productive cherry orchards in all of Europe.

Nelson continued to run the Orchard. He also met and fell in love with a girl in the village, whom he eventually married.

Patin worked at the Orchard, remaining in charge of packing and shipping. He lived in a small cabin with his dog, Deba, whom he brought to work with him every day.

Cura had a child and became a teacher at the only school in the village. She loved her job. And because gypsy tradition had it that the females in the family were the only ones able to perform the *dukkering*, Cura was given her mother's Crystal Ball which she proudly kept displayed on the mantle of her fireplace.

Clopin spent his time in the village with old friends, playing chess and sipping his favorite wine.

Next to the Guru Sylvanus, Clopin was regarded as the village's wisest man. And others often came to him for his advice.

The Guru Sylvanus had become quite frail by this time and was unable to get into the village except for its once a year New Year's Eve celebration, which he wouldn't miss no matter how he felt. To get there he would have someone help him to the village where he would join in the celebration by having one drink and watching the others dance and sing until he tired out and had to be brought home.

Grinza's favorite cherry tree was still doing well, in the front yard of the first cabin her parents had built - the same cabin in which Pali and Cura now lived. The neighborhood children were always invited to pick the cherries when they were ripe, and Pali and Cura enjoyed watching the children playing under the tree and hearing them yell out how many cherries they had picked.

Exactly one year after Grinza's death, something happened that the villagers would speak of for many, many years to come; in fact, the story of this event spread far and wide, becoming part of the history and lore of the village forever after.

For the villagers, that day went by much as any other. People went to work; their children went to school. After work that day, Clopin and his children got together to reminisce about Grinza. They told each other funny and poignant stories and they laughed and cried together as they spoke of her. When it started to get dark, they each went their separate ways, feeling a bit sad, but happy they had been able to be together.

Then it happened. It was like a fantasy, a fairy tale, but it was real. At exactly nine o'clock in the evening, all at once, every streetlight in the village went dark. It was as if it had gone from daylight to darkness in a flash. Everyone ran out from their homes to find out what had happened, but it was so dark outside that they couldn't see more than a few feet in front of them.

Everyone was frightened. Some children cried. And then, as if someone had turned on a switch, all the lights came back on. And the shock of what they saw left everyone in silence. Looking up and down the street, they saw that every single cherry tree in the village, including Grinza's favorite, the entire orchard and everyone else's, were covered with brilliant pink cherry blossoms... in September. This was impossible! There was snow on the ground. The cherry blossoms only came out in the spring.

"How," they wondered. "How did this happen?"

But they all knew that this magical appearance of the cherry blossoms, on the exact date of the one-year anniversary of Grinza's death, was not only a miracle, but also a sign. A gift to the village in remembrance of the special and oh so loved Grinza! And they looked toward the darkened sky and could picture Grinza, a big smile on her face, looking down at them, at her orchard, at all the cherry blossoms, and at the village she so loved.

CPSIA information can be obtained
at www.ICGtesting.com
Printed in the USA
LVHW071304140520
655613LV00025B/2318

9 781977 223524